Run Fast, Fly Far

written by Beth Terrill

illustrated by Rachael Phillips

McGraw-Hill
School Division

New York   Farmington

Kenu and his friend Miko were running on the beach when they saw a tiny bird sitting all alone in the sand. It had no feathers yet. Its skin was pink and it was moving little wings.

"That's the funniest–looking bird I've ever seen," said Miko.

"Oh, I think it's kind of cute. I bet it's just a baby," guessed Kenu, looking around. "I don't see its mother anywhere."

At that moment, two gulls swooped down toward the little bird. So, Kenu gently picked up the bird and put it in his hat.

He could argue with his coach later, but for now track practice would have to wait.

Kenu was happy to have his very own pet bird. He named the bird Jesse, in honor of his favorite track star, Jesse Owens.

They walked to First Avenue and took Jesse to the community pet store. He looked hungry! So, they wanted to buy him some bird food.

Inside the pet shop, they saw beautiful green parrots and yellow canaries. None of the birds looked like their Jesse.

"Do you have any food for baby birds?" Kenu asked the shopkeeper. Jesse squealed from Kenu's hat, so Kenu took him out.

The shopkeeper replied, "You could use cat food mixed with water, but if I were you I'd take that bird to Elaine's Farm. She runs a nursery for little wild birds."

Kenu thought about what the shopkeeper said. Because he wanted to take care of Jesse himself, Kenu took Jesse home.

Kenu and Miko soon discovered that feeding a baby bird wasn't easy. When Kenu tried to dribble a little cat food into Jesse's mouth, Jesse wiggled and moved his wings.

Miko laughed and followed Kenu out the door. He knew where they were headed. They were taking Jesse to Elaine's Farm.

Elaine ran out to meet Kenu and Miko. "That's an Arctic tern!" she cried, when she saw Jesse. "These birds fly farther than any bird on Earth."

"At the end of August, when it starts to get cold here in Canada, she'll migrate almost 10,000 miles to the South Pole. Then, when it gets to be winter in the South Pole, she'll come back here in June, just in time for our summer.

"Hey, wait a minute. Jesse's a girl?"

But, boy or girl, Kenu didn't like the idea of turning Jesse loose so soon.

Elaine placed Jesse in a small box with a blanket and a heater. "I don't want to worry you," said Elaine, "but Jesse seems really weak. She may not be ready to go in four weeks with the other terns."

Four weeks wasn't long. In four weeks, Kenu and Miko would be running six miles in the town race. That was nothing compared to a commute of 10,000 miles.

Kenu was glad that Jesse would be around for a while. He continued to visit her at Elaine's every day. At each visit Jesse looked a little different.

Now Jesse was in a bigger cage. She was covered in fluffy, white feathers. She looked like a powder-puff on skinny red legs. She was also starting to walk. She'd take a few wobbly steps, then fall over.

"She doesn't look like she could fly 10,000 miles," said Miko.

Kenu just smiled and watched Jesse's movements. He had seen how much and how fast Jesse had improved already.

Elaine had a few other birds but no Arctic terns, like Jesse.

"We really need to set Jesse free as soon as she is mature enough. She needs to learn from other Arctic terns how to dive for fish," said Elaine.

Kenu felt bad that Jesse was all alone.

"You've got to eat, so you'll get stronger," whispered Kenu, watching Jesse closely.

Jesse was now eating sardines and shrimp. She walked proudly on her webbed feet and poked at Kenu's fingers with her sharp, pointy beak. It looked as if she were trying to prove to him how strong she was getting.

"Ouch!" cried Kenu. "You'll have no trouble catching your own fish with that beak," he assured Jesse. "Believe me!"

"Why do Arctic terns fly so far?" Kenu asked Elaine one afternoon.

"They would die during our cold winters. They also need to leave to find food," said Elaine. "Jesse will spend most of her life in the air and see more sunshine than any other animal."

"Wow," said Miko, as he came in. Miko knew he'd find his friend at Elaine's.

"I'm going on vacation for two weeks," said Miko. "I'll be back just in time for the race. Don't spend all your time with that bird. Include a little time to train for your *own* race!"

Kenu smiled. He liked spending his time at Elaine's with Jesse, but he knew what his friend was saying was absolutely true.

When Jesse had lots of long feathers, Elaine moved her into a huge cage with trees, rocks, and two baby ospreys.

"Now that Jesse's bigger, I think she needs to be around other birds," explained Elaine.

Jesse puffed up her feathers when she saw the other birds. As Jesse walked past one of them, it raised its jagged claw. Squawk! Jesse was cornered.

"Get away from her!" yelled Kenu, trying to open the cage. The door was stuck!

To Kenu's surprise, Jesse flew to the other side of the cage. When had she learned to fly?

By the time Miko came back, Jesse had all of her feathers. She was much bigger. From one end of her wings to the other, Jesse was as long as Kenu's arm. She flew around the cage as if she'd always known how to fly. Kenu thought she was really beautiful.

"That's Jesse?" asked Miko, with his mouth open.

Kenu laughed and said, "She's been practicing for her race. Did you practice for *yours*?"

"Did *you*?" asked Miko right back. Both boys laughed with good humor. They knew they were not as ready for their race as they hoped Jesse was for hers.

As the summer days got shorter, the terns began to leave. Elaine told the boys she'd set Jesse loose early the next day—if Jesse chose to go.

Kenu and Miko stayed the night at the farm, so they could be there in the morning.

"I think she's going to do it," said Kenu, watching Jesse fly back and forth.

The sun was rising when Elaine woke Kenu and Miko. Kenu threw Jesse some fish for breakfast. Then he opened the large door of the cage.

At first Jesse didn't seem to notice the cage was open. Was it the gentle ocean breeze that called to her? It was only a few moments before Jesse flew out. Kenu and Miko watched the tern fly into the sky, and then land on a branch in a nearby tree.

"She's looking at us," said Kenu.

"She's saying thank you," said Miko.

Then, joining the other terns, Jesse beat her wings in unison with them as they flew south.

The boys thanked Elaine and said good-bye. Then they ran over to the track. Their own race was due to start in thirty minutes.

"Jesse's got a long way to go," said Kenu, watching some birds on the horizon.

"Ten-thousand miles? That's nothing," said Miko with a laugh. "We've got to go *six* miles *without* wings."

Miko and Kenu ran their fastest. . . but they didn't finish first, second, or even tenth. But they did cross the finish line.

Would Jesse cross hers and come back next summer? The boys promised one another to watch for Jesse then.